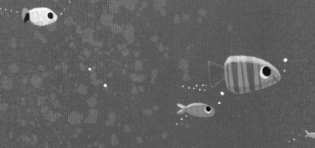

For everyone out there brave
enough to try ~ T.C.

For Mom and Dad and all
that you do ~ T.N.

tiger tales

5 River Road, Suite 128, Wilton, CT 06897
Published in the United States 2020
Originally published in Great Britain 2020
by Little Tiger Press Ltd.
Text copyright © 2020 Tracey Corderoy
Illustrations copyright © 2020 Tony Neal
ISBN-13: 978-1-68010-191-1
ISBN-10: 1-68010-191-9
Printed in China
LTP/1400/2941/0919

For more insight and activities,
visit us at www.tigertalesbooks.com

IT'S IMPOSSIBLE!

by Tracey Corderoy

Illustrated by Tony Neal

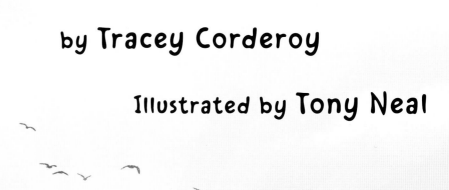

tiger tales

On the sunniest street, in the busiest city,
Dog ran a neat little laundry service.
He whistled as he washed his customers' clothes
and hung them on the rooftop to dry.

ocean wash

Laundry service

But the city was noisy, even at night.
At bedtime, Dog turned on his ocean nightlight.
It filled his dreams with the soft, gentle swish of the sea.

If only he could visit the real ocean.
But it was just too far away . . . .

Instead, Dog made little boats
and read thrilling ocean tales.

Then one day, he discovered a
brand-new laundry soap . . . .

"Ocean Magic!
For seaside freshness
with every wash!"

He couldn't wait to try it out!

Dog poured in the laundry soap, and the clothes began to swirl.

Soon, the smell of the ocean filled the air. "Magical!" Dog smiled. It felt like he was really there.

Then Dog heard something.

"A crab?" he cried.
"It's impossible!"

"Ugh!" groaned
the crab.
"I feel sick!"

"How did you get here,
Crab?" Dog asked.
Crab shrugged. "One minute
I was on my beach—
then, like magic, I was in
your laundry basket!"

After a few minutes, Crab said,
"It's time to go home.
Can I borrow your bike?"
"Of course," agreed Dog. "But
will your feet reach the pedals?"

"So, mail me instead," tried Crab.
"You'd get squashed!"
sputtered Dog.
"Then I'll walk," announced
Crab, scuttling to the door.

"Wait—it's MILES," gasped Dog. "Look!"
He pointed to a map on the wall and sighed.
"I've always wanted to go to the ocean.
But it's too far to drive. It's impossible."

"I've got it!" beamed Crab. "Let's drive
there TOGETHER. A road trip. It'll be fun!"
"I'm not sure," began Dog. But he really wanted
to see the ocean, and help Crab, too.

Dog listened to Crab's plan.
"Let's do it," he said finally.

Early the next day, Dog hopped in the van to deliver his customers' clothes. But when he got back, his suitcase was all packed!

Dog gasped. It was one thing to SAY he would go, but quite another to actually DO it.

"It's **impossible**," he said sadly. "I can't leave. I'm sorry."

"It's only impossible if you say it is," replied Crab. "Can't we try?"

And so they did!
"We're off!" cheered Dog.
This road trip just might be possible after all.

START
CITY

REALLY HIGH!

Dog and Crab traveled for weeks.
They drove through dark caves
and crossed giant waterfalls.
And every day, they added
special memories to
their map.

EEK!

RICKETY BRIDGE!!

CAVES

NATURE HIKE

DARK CAVE!

Then one day, they climbed a mountain to the top of the world!

"Oh, Crab!" exclaimed Dog. "I never knew there was so much to see."

They met others on their own journeys, too.

"I used to be scared of heights," Mouse smiled. "But look at me now— right up here!"

"Only if you say it is," chuckled Dog. And together, they had the tent up in no time!

That night, Dog and Crab were warm and snug as the wind howled around them.

By morning, all was calm . . .

"And I always got frustrated easily," said Flamingo. "But now I can do anything. Except put up tents on windy mountains. That's IMPOSSIBLE!"

. . . but the road to the ocean was blocked!

Dog and Crab had come so far.
"We can move that tree, can't we, Crab?" asked Dog.
"We'll finish our journey, won't we?"

But Crab knew that this time,
it really was impossible.
"Dog, the thing is," he began,
when . . .

VROOOOM!
It was Flamingo in her monster truck.
"Let's get this tree out of here!" she called.

Soon Dog and Crab were on their way again.
"Follow that seaside breeze!" said Crab.
So they did just that, on and on until . . .

"The ocean!" exclaimed Dog.
"Home!" cheered Crab. "We did it,
Dog—we DID it!"

At last, it was time to explore . . . .

Dog flew kites, jumped waves,
and built castles in the sand.

And the pale blue fish that once
flickered from his nightlight
now swam around him in all the
colors of the rainbow!

Dog wished he could stay forever. But every vacation has to end.

"I have to go back," he sighed, "to my job and my home." "But you love it here!" cried Crab.

Dog nodded. "But to stay is imposs—" Then he stopped. "It's only impossible if I SAY it is . . . ," gasped Dog.

On the sunniest beach, by the
calmest ocean, Dog and Crab now
run the most magical café.
And together, NOTHING feels impossible!